THE DAY I GOT ZAPPED WITH SUPER POWERS

Other titles by Tom McLaughlin:

The Day that Aliens Nearly Ate our Brains

The Day I Became the Most Wanted Boy in the World

The Day I Found a Wormhole at the Bottom of the Garden

The Day I Started a Mega Robot Invasion

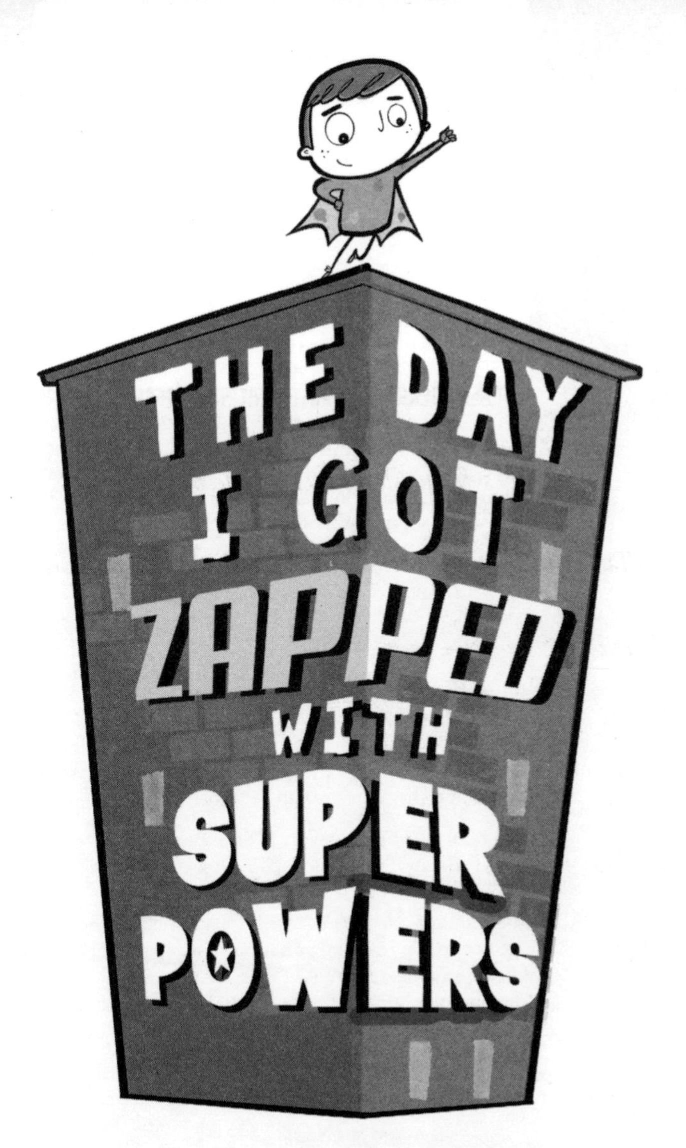

TOM McLAUGHLIN

WALKER
BOOKS

This is a work of fiction. Names, characters, places and incidents are either the product of the author's imagination or, if real, used fictitiously. All statements, activities, stunts, descriptions, information and material of any other kind contained herein are included for entertainment purposes only and should not be relied on for accuracy or replicated as they may result in injury.

First published in Great Britain 2021 by Walker Books Ltd
87 Vauxhall Walk, London SE11 5HJ

2 4 6 8 10 9 7 5 3 1

This book has been typeset in Stempel Schneidler

Printed and bound by CPI Group (UK) Ltd, Croydon CR0 4YY

British Library Cataloguing in Publication Data:
a catalogue record for this book is available from the British Library

ISBN 978-1-4063-8965-4

www.walker.co.uk

Activities are for informational and/or entertainment purposes only.

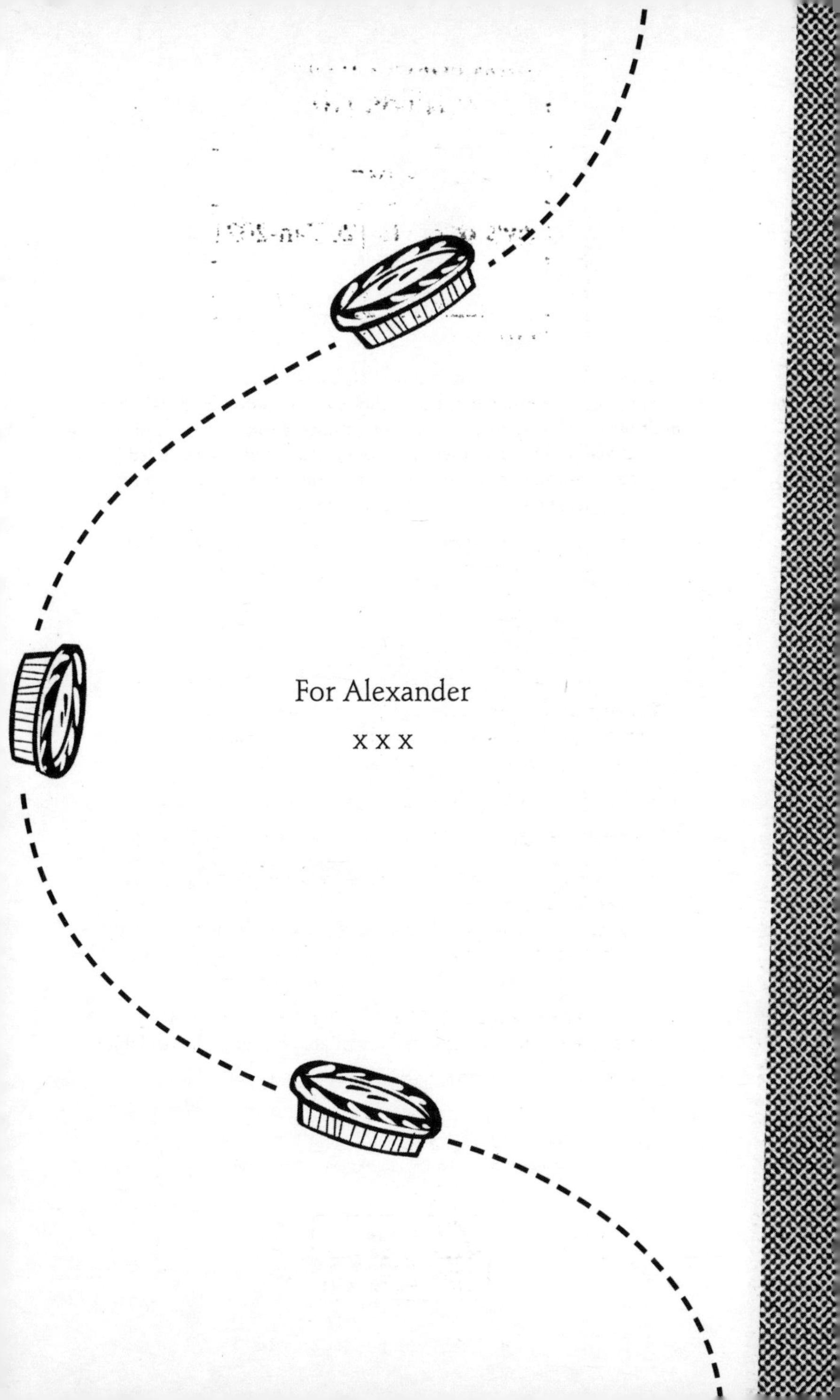

For Alexander

x x x

1 p.m.

"At last, we meet again, Doctor Dangerous."

"Untie me, you fiend! One of these days, Splendid Man, I'll make you pay for this!"

"Cash or cheque? MWA-HA-HA!*"*

"Let me go, or the whole world will know your secret..."

"You mean...?"

"Yes, your BIRTH name. Given to you as a hairless sprog!"

"YOU'RE BLUFFING!"

"LET ME GO, SPLENDID MAN, OR EVERYONE WILL KNOW THAT YOUR REAL NAME IS—"

"HARRY RAMSBOTTOM!"

"What?" Harry said, glancing up from his comic.

"Harry Ramsbottom, are you listening to a word I say? Put down your *Splendid Man* comic and listen up. We're nearly there. I don't know how you even read on the bus – it makes me feel very bilious."

"What does 'bilious' mean?" Harry asked his grandad.

"It's like sick," Grandad replied.

"Well, why don't you just say 'sick', then?" Harry asked.

"I've got a new app that sends me a

word every day. I was trying to work it into the conversation. 'Bilious' was a good deal easier than yesterday's, I tell you."

"What was that?"

"'Duck-billed platypus'. You just don't see that many round Basingstoke, not these days." Grandad sighed, dinging the bell and lighting up the "stop" sign. "Right, have you got your money?"

"YES!" Harry said, tapping his top pocket.

"Maybe you could buy a new notebook for the bestselling comic you're going to write? How's that going by the way?" Grandad asked casually as the bus came to a hissing stop.

"I wish I hadn't said anything," Harry muttered. "I'm still in the planning stage," he said more loudly as they stepped off the bus.

Harry desperately wanted to be a comic book writer but he was having a hard time getting started.

"How far have you got? Title, chapters, sketches?" Grandad continued as they walked along the high street.

"Grandad!" Harry snapped. "Leave it,

it'll be ready when it's ready. I'm just trying to find a good idea."

"All right, all right. Now, I've got a few things to pick up in town. Are you OK to get back home from here?"

"Grandad! What do you take me for?"

"Remember to catch the Number 14 from the right side of the road this time."

"I only made that mistake once! You've got to let it go, Grandad." Harry shook his head.

"Fine. Just be careful! What do you want for tea?"

"Meat pie!" Harry yelled instantly.

"A fine choice, sir. It'll be ... *ahem* ... splendiferous..."

"Word of the day again?"

"Yep, it's the app that keeps on giving.

Pies it is! Take care, Hal. See you later," Grandad said, blowing him a kiss.

Harry waved his grandad goodbye before making his weekly pilgrimage down the high street to the comic shop. It was where you'd find him every Saturday afternoon, without fail. Some kids went to football, others lay about in their PJs eating cereal and playing video games, but, for Harry, his most favourite thing in the world was finding new comics to read for the rest of the week. Then, come Saturday, it was time to repeat the whole thing again. Back home, he'd read them, reread them, look at the pictures, tidy them, put them in order, dust them, put them in a different order … and so on. Often he'd bring them into school to show his mates at lunchtime – if it was a particularly good edition or if there was something really special about it, like a cool drawing.

That was the other thing Harry liked to do: copy the drawings. He was working on his own idea for a comic, but he just didn't have quite the right story yet. And well, there was the other thing too … he wasn't so good at spelling.

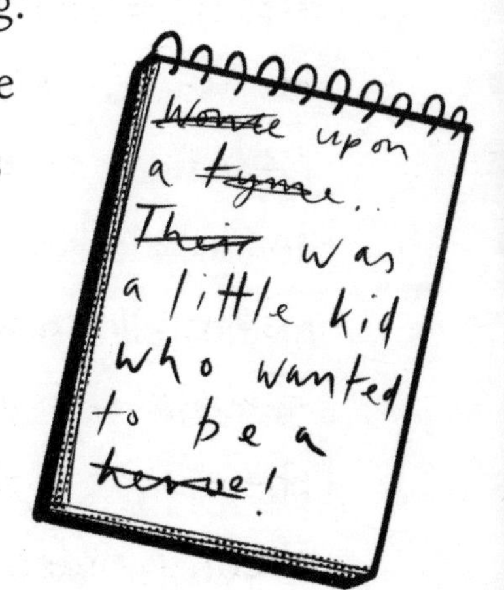

Whenever he had to write anything in school, his work would always come back splattered with red corrections, looking like the teacher had had a nosebleed all over it. He tried his best, but he found words difficult. He was beginning to think he should just stick to *reading* comics and let the people who were good at words write them.

Harry took a deep sigh and scuffed his trainers on the pavement; the coins in his pocket jingled. He got pocket money for doing various things for his grandad during the week: putting the bins out, helping to feed the fish, finding Grandad's glasses – he was always taking them off and leaving them somewhere weird, like the loo. Harry had wondered whether he should tell Grandad to buy one of those spectacle chain things, but that would cut Harry's pocket money by about forty-five per cent, so he just kept quiet.

The high street was busy so Harry

decided to take a shortcut. There was a narrow alleyway that went round the back of the shops. No one else used it even though it was faster – it was super-creepy. Opposite the shop walls was a looming wire fence topped with sharp spikes to stop anyone climbing in and going where they weren't wanted. Behind the razor-sharp fence stood a really strange warehouse-like building. It looked like it had been taken straight from Gotham City and dropped in the middle of Basingstoke. The windows were steamed up and misty so you couldn't see in. The bricks were almost black, as if the whole thing had been carved out of coal. It didn't have any signs on it – apart from one: *TRESPASSERS WILL BE PROSECUTED*

No one ever saw anyone come or go. No one really knew what it was for or what people did in there but, whatever it was and whoever they were, they clearly didn't want anyone to find out. Harry always ran past the building – it made his spine shiver and tingle like his bones were made of ice. He never stopped.

He never looked too closely. He just ran until the fence disappeared and he was back among the shops and people again. It gave him the heebie-jeebies, but that was a small price to pay for getting to the comic shop that little bit quicker. Just before he was about to make a run for it, he felt something brush against him.

"Oh, hello," he said, looking down as a cat snaked between his legs. "What are you doing sneaking around? Well, I don't have anything for you. No snacks, I'm afraid," Harry said, giving the cat a tickle before he legged it as fast as he could through the alleyway.

DING-A-LING! The bell rang as he opened the door to the comic shop. Harry took a deep sniff and savoured the smell of ink on paper. "Ah, my people!" he thought as he gazed around the shop at his fellow nerdlings. A few lifted their heads from the shelves and stared back. Harry sometimes forgot that his thoughts came out as words. And that's when he saw it – the latest issue of *Splendid Man*. Harry ran over and grabbed it. His eyes gobbled up every bit of the cover like he was about to have it for tea. He went to turn the first page but stopped himself. "No! You'll enjoy it more if you wait," he muttered.

"'Course I know what goes on in there.

Everyone knows." Harry overheard a couple of older teens talking on the other side of the shelf.

"You don't know!" the girl with the pigtails scoffed.

"Listen, I saw someone go in there once. He had, like, a MASSIVE laser thing."

"The building out back?" the other guy asked.

"Yeah. I swear it's an Area 51-type place – highly classified – where they do all these weird experiments. Like spawning aliens to take over the planet and stuff."

"You're talking a load of baloney," the girl sneered.

"No, seriously, I read it on the Internet."

"Oh, *the Internet*… Then maybe it *is* true…"

Harry stood on his tiptoes, listening hard for more details, but the group of teens had gone. *Were they definitely talking about the building in the alleyway?* he thought to himself. *Alien stuff? No, surely not?*

Harry glanced at the clock. If he bought his comics now, maybe he could go and watch for a while. Well, maybe not watch, but walk past really, really slowly – see if anyone went in... *You couldn't get into trouble for just looking, could you?* Perhaps this was just what he needed to help him write his comic – intel on super-secret aliens. It wasn't spying if he was doing research for a book. Where was the harm in that?

2 p.m.

Harry paid for his comics, put them in his bag along with the receipt, and headed back the way he'd come down the alleyway. This time, instead of quickening his pace as he usually did, he stopped in front of the building and stared up at it. Harry wasn't really sure what he was looking for: something out of place maybe, a flash at the window, or even a UFO landing on the roof – yes, that would be definite proof that something weird was going on. Harry glanced up at the sky as the roar of a jumbo jet flew above him. When the noise died down, he heard something: a clank of metal and … was that footsteps, too? He squinted, cocked his head and tried to do his best listening. He was trying to figure out where the noise was coming from when suddenly he felt something land on his shoulder.

"AGGGGGGGGH!"

he yelled,
leaping about
three metres
in the air!

"Miaooow." It was the cat from before. It had sprung out of nowhere and was now digging its claws into Harry's favourite jumper.

"Do not do that! You scared me half to DEATH!" Harry bellowed, his heart beating like a drum in his chest. The cat gave him a sideways glance and jumped off his shoulder. "I told you, I don't have anything for you. What are you, some sort of guard cat?" Harry asked suspiciously. The cat glared back at him. *I mean he did look pretty scary*, Harry thought, as he got into a staring competition. The cat thought better of it and fell asleep right there and then. *Maybe he wasn't such a good guard cat after all.*

Harry looked over at the building again,

then checked the time and yawned. This research thing was, if truth be told, a little boring. He had been there for nearly ten minutes and hadn't seen a single laser or UFO. "Right, well, I'm off out of here, strange goings on or not. I'm going home to read these beauties and maybe have a pie. It's past my lunchtime – enough of this sloping about business." Harry said to himself.

"Miaooow," the cat responded, waking up and following Harry.

"Sorry, mate, not enough pie for two," he said, turning round. "No, seriously, you can't follow me home. Go on, shooooo…" Harry flapped his hands at the cat, but it was useless. I mean is there anything more futile than telling a cat what to do?

"Please, Whatever Your Name Is, just hop it..." Harry thought for a second. *What don't cats like ... they don't like dogs, that's a fact. It's in all the cartoons.* So Harry decided that the best thing to do would be ...

"RUUUUUUFFFF!"

"MIAOOOOOOWWWWW
WWOOOOOOW!"

the cat squealed and ran straight up the fence towards the dark building.

"Oh, no, stop! You'll get stuck! Come back." *What had he done?* Harry tried to entice the cat back over the fence, but the more he tried, the further it walked away. Harry had a serious dilemna. What if the cat was abducted and made into alien stew? It would be all his fault. Rescuing a stray cat had *really* not been on his to-do list for the day. In fact, Harry much preferred reading about heroic acts than doing them himself but what choice did he have?

"Right..." Harry said, steeling himself. "Here we go..." And with a bit of pushing and shoving – and a very scary incident at the top where he nearly got cut in two – he managed to get over the fence and into the grounds. The strange building seemed to grow twice the size. Close up, it was also twice as scary.

"Come back!" he whisper-yelled at the cat. But with every step he took, the cat walked further away from him. Spotting another *TRESPASSERS WILL BE PROSECTUED* sign, Harry felt a wave of nausea wash over him. This was by far the most dangerous and most stupid thing he'd ever done. "Great, now I need a wee!" he called after the cat.

That's how nerves expressed themselves in Harry – through his bladder. The school play, for instance, would be a five-wee type of situation. A maths exam, while still nerve-wracking, would only be a two-wee problem, say. This, however, was definitely a ten-wee scenario. The cat disappeared round the corner so Harry followed too, crawling on his hands and knees, making the sort of lip-smacking squeaky sounds one does when trying to get a cat to come to you. He crept round the corner, making sure that no one was

about. It suddenly went deadly quiet; the distant din of traffic was gone and now there was just an eerie silence – and no cat.

"Pusskins … I'm sorry about the barking thing. That was a mean trick. Please come out! Maybe we can share that pie after all…" he cajoled, pulling out his ace card. Then Harry noticed a huge garage-like door, the sort you pull up from the bottom. A garage-like door that was now just open enough for a cat to creep through – a cat and a very small boy. "Oh, fine. I mean, why not?" Harry sighed. "I've probably already broken the law. I can't *believe* I'm going to be experimented on by aliens – all to save a cat that isn't even mine." Harry took a deep breath, before pulling himself through the small gap on his hands and knees.

It was dark and it seemed to take an age for his eyes to adjust. As the cavernous room began to take shape, he thought he saw something in the distance. "Pusskins…?" he called. There was a miaow then a crash of metal and a shriek from the cat that sounded far away.

"OK, OK, OK, OK. I'm coming…" Harry said, putting his hands out to feel for a light switch. He took hold of a lever … a lever is like a switch, isn't it? After a second's pause, he gave it a sharp yank. Suddenly, one by one, lights began to turn on and Harry could finally see where he was. It was some sort of warehouse laid out like a huge laboratory with machines everywhere.

"There you are...!" Harry said, spotting the cat. Harry held out his hands but the terrified cat ran straight past him towards the door without giving him a second glance. "Oh, you're welcome!" Harry cried out sarcastically after it. He shook his head as the cat disappeared. But any worries about the moggy were soon replaced with new ones.

"What is that?" Harry asked aloud as he heard a high-pitched whining sound. It was getting louder and louder, like something was warming up, something big and electronic. Suddenly, there was a rumble as a trapdoor opened in the floor and a giant satellite dish type-thing popped out. The machines around the room began to bleep and dials began to turn. "Erm... Hey,

Siri, turn everything off!" Harry yelled out in desperation. Nothing happened. "Well, it was a long shot, I guess," he sighed.

Harry was in two minds. Should he try and fix things or run? Harry looked at the strange machine. It wasn't a satellite dish after all. He reached into his bag and held up his *Splendid Man* comic. There on the front cover was a giant laser, exactly like the one in front of him. "Oh my days! It's what those guys were talking about in the shop." *Run!!!* Harry thought.

JUST RUN!

He dropped the comic and legged it as fast as he could towards the door. But before he could make it out, there was a bright flash of light and a deafening scream. An indescribable pain shot through him – as if he'd been struck on the bottom by lightning. Then everything went black.

3 p.m.

"What on earth?" Harry said, coming round. "What's that burning smell…?" He rubbed his head and looked over his shoulder. "Wait, that's my bottom! My bottom is on fire!" Harry screamed, spinning around in a circle, doing a good impression of a human Catherine wheel.

"Ow, ow, OWWWW!" he yelled, galloping up and down looking for a fire extinguisher, a bucket of water, an old

cup of coffee, anything! "This is a health and safety nightmare," Harry muttered under his breath,

"Hang on, fire needs oxygen. Yes, that's it! I need to starve the fire of oxygen," he thought out loud as the only thing he remembered from science came flooding back.

"A BIN SHOULD DO IT!"

He spotted a small dustbin and quickly sat down on it like it was a potty. Miraculously, it worked! But then Harry remembered the only *other* thing he'd learnt in science: when you remove air from a confined space, you create a vacuum. In other words …

"Oh, come on! Now I've got a bin stuck on my bum! What else could possibly go wrong?" Just then, the smoke hit the detectors and the sprinklers came on, raining down on Harry. "Oh, perfect!" he cried out. "Well, at least it can't get any worse." He took a deep breath … and it got worse.

WAAAH WAAAH WAAAAH!

Alarms started wailing and flashing red, lighting up the whole building. Soaking wet, with a small dustbin stuck on his burnt bottom, Harry decided that his work here was done. He made a dash for the door. Not an easy task with a bin on your bum.

Harry scampered across the soaking wet floor like a human hermit crab on the run. As soon as he got to the door, Harry crouched down and used his crab legs to push himself sideways through the small gap. He made it!

The sirens were as deafening outside as they were inside and he probably only had a few minutes before the police or fire brigade turned up, and then he'd be in big trouble. Harry needed to get out of there fast. He tried grabbing the bin off his bum but it was just too stuck. If only there was a way to propel it off...

That's when it hit him: what if he guffed? Would a well-aimed bottom burp shoot the bin off his butt? Harry looked around. There was no way he would be able to make it over the fence with a bin on his bum, let alone catch a bus, without attracting attention. No, it was not a question of whether he should try. The real question was: could he summon one up? If he was Billy from geography, things would be different. That kid could fart on request – he seemed to have an

endless supply. But Harry, being the well-brought-up boy he was, didn't tend to let rip with carefree abandon. But these were desperate times, so, using all his strength, he closed his eyes and thought windy thoughts, and released a gust to beat all gusts. The thunder from down below shot the bin off with all the velocity of a cannonball. Harry turned to see it fly towards the fence and flinched as it embedded among the wires.

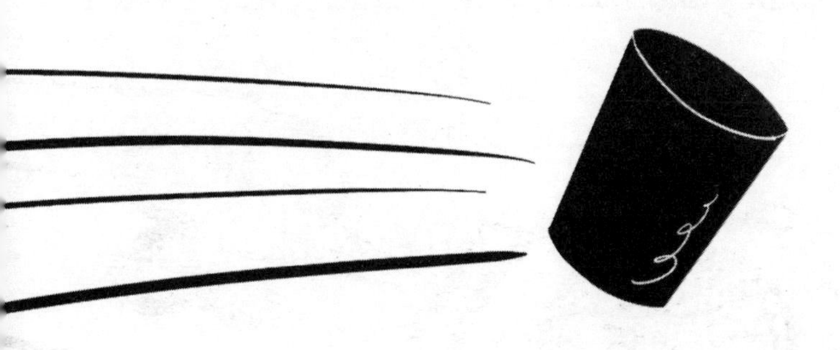

"That's the last time I'm having bran flakes for breakfast..." he said in amazement. He didn't have long to admire his handiwork, as a black car came screeching round the side of the building. Harry's plan of escaping without anyone noticing was kaput. He looked at the car and looked at the fence, could he make it? The car doors swung open and a man and a woman jumped out. They were both dressed in black suits and sunglasses. They didn't look like police; they looked exactly like secret agents or worse – the baddies from his comic books.

"DON'T MOVE!"

the woman yelled.

Harry wasn't going to stick around.

"I just wanted to help a lost cat! Sorry, it was an accideeeeent!" he cried out.

"What was an accident?" the man shouted.

"I've got to go. Sorry again!" Harry cried out apologetically.

"DO NOT MOVE!" the woman in black yelled again, before sprinting towards Harry.

Harry looked at the fence and then at the people chasing him. He began to run, faster than he'd ever run before in his life. The ground disappeared beneath his feet. It was the most incredible feeling, like his legs weren't his own. Looking over his shoulder, he realized he was beating the grown-ups: this made no sense. He got to the fence and climbed it like a spider scampering over a web. Who knew that being chased by baddies in dark glasses would have improved his PE skills? Harry jumped down the other side and ran along the alleyway. He glanced back to see the two baddies attempt to climb over the fence and chase him down. They managed it with far less finesse than Harry. Once they'd landed, Harry saw the woman head in the direction of the comic shop while the man was in hot pursuit after him. Harry was just about to turn into the crowded high street where he'd be safe when he saw the female agent appear in front of him. Harry spun on his heels, only to find he was cornered.

"Give it up, kid. It's over. All we want to do is help." The man attempted a weak smile.

"Leave me alone!" Harry cried out.

"Stay still, kid. We wouldn't want you to get hurt," the woman said reassuringly.

"Leave me alone or I'll call the—"

"Police? They can't help you," the man said. "Only we can."

Looking up, Harry saw a drainpipe high above his head. There was nothing to lose. He closed his eyes and jumped the biggest jump he could jump. When he opened his eyes again, he saw the shop window ledge sailing past – he was still jumping! He looked down below as the two agents gasped in amazement. He looked up to the sky – he was still going, higher and higher! Was this jumping or flying? At what point does one become the other? He looked down and waved a sarcastic wave.

"Catch you later!" he said, sailing over the top of the shop buildings and above the town.

Whatever it was that had just happened, things would never be the same again.

"I can fly!" he shouted. "Uh-oh…" His

stomach lurched. "Oh my…" The trouble with flying was that it always made Harry very, very sick.

BLEURGH!

He sent one flying. "Watch oooouuuut below!"

Yes, things would never be the same again – especially for the traffic warden finishing his shift beneath.

4 p.m.

After recovering from his bout of air-sickness, Harry soon got used to the idea that he could fly. It was all in the mind. Harry thought back to the incident with the bin. He had just closed his eyes and imagined the parp – and the bin had flown off like a rocket. It was the same when he'd scarpered over the fence. All he'd had to do was imagine a skill and it happened. It was the same with flying. If he thought

about turning left, he did. The same with turning right, swooping or going up – even loop-the-looping probably, but Harry made a mental note not to try that until there was no one below (just in case he got sick again).

"Right, I can fly around all day but, as much fun as this is, people might start to notice a low-flying boy," Harry said to himself. "I need to go home and tell Grandad that I'm now, you know, a superhero."

After flying through the clouds with his mouth open, just for fun – well, who wouldn't want to taste the clouds? – he scanned the land below. He couldn't quite

work out where he was. Things looked different from above. "I think I'm lost!" Harry said, coming to a hovering stop in mid-air. "Wait, is that the Number 14 bus?" Harry looked down as the traffic meandered along the roads. "I think it is! I know what to do…"

Over the next twenty minutes, Harry flew above the bus, following every stop and turn. When it went around the roundabout, so did Harry. If it pulled over, so did Harry. Then, before he knew it, the bus screeched to a halt right outside the small house he shared with his grandad.

Harry waited until it was quiet and, when no one was looking, came to a gentle landing outside McTucky Fried Chicken. Harry felt unsteady on his feet for a few seconds – the way you do when you get off a rollercoaster. Harry strolled along his street, same as always, but everything looked and felt different. He couldn't stop smiling. He had secret powers, and it felt good.

"Grandad!" Harry said, bursting in through the front door. "I need to tell you something – it's massive!"

"Wait up!" Grandad said. "Steak and kidney or minced beef?"

"THIS IS MORE IMPORTANT THAN PIES!"

Harry yelled.

Grandad gasped and looked at Harry in disbelief.

"Sorry, Grandad! I shouldn't have said that. I was out of order," Harry said, apologizing.

"OK, but don't ever say that again! Pies are great; pies will always be great. A pie won't let you down. Friends may come and go, but pies…"

"I know. But can I tell you something? It's really important," Harry said.

"What is it?" Grandad asked, looking concerned. "Is everything OK?"

"Yes, everything's fine..." Harry said, pausing. He hadn't really thought about how to say this. "I mean, well ... I farted a bin off and set my bum on fire but on the bright side, I can fly now."

"What?"

"Sorry, that came out a bit confused. I'll work backwards... No, backwards isn't good. I'll work forwards, but a really quick version."

"HARRY!"

"Sorry. OK, I think I got shot by this weird laser in this really scary building and now I have superpowers. I didn't catch the bus home; I flew. I can fly now, and also run really fast and jump incredibly high and fart with the strength of a hundred men – although that may just have been the bran flakes."

"Sit down and start from the very beginning," Grandad said.

Ten minutes later, Harry and Grandad stood in the garden.

"In your own time," Grandad said, with a look on his face as if to say, *Oh reaaaally now?* which was totally understandable.

"OK, I can prove it," Harry said, shaking his head, hands and feet as if he was warming up for the high jump. He fixed his eyes on the clouds and took a deep breath. "Oh boy, I really hope this works."

"Me, too. If you're making this up and we've got cold pies for nothing, then, heaven help me, I won't be held responsible for my actions!"

"Three … two … one…" Harry said, closing his eyes and jumping high into the air.

"Oh my! You're doing it!" Grandad gasped. "Is this a magic trick? I know they sell those in that fancy-dress shop in town."

"They sell tricks with fake dog poo, Grandad! Not tricks that make you fly! No, this is all me, I told you. Look at my trousers. Scorch marks! The laser got me and this is what happened."

"Incredible! Do you know what this means?"

"No, what?"

"I'm not sure, but it's got to be good. Fly higher."

"OK, but I don't want to go up too high."

"In case you throw up again?" Grandad asked.

"Noooo. Well, not just that. I don't want too many people to see."

"Higher!" Grandad said, waving his arms.

"OK..."

"Now lower..."

"Erm, here?" Harry asked, hovering to a stop.

"Yes! Right, while you're up there, can you take all those dead leaves out of the gutter?"

"Are you using my new-formed super-powers to clear the roof?!" Harry yelled.

"Listen, it was going to cost me thirty pounds to get those cleared! Now you can do it for free."

"I bet Splendid Man doesn't have to put up with this: 'Sorry, I can't save the world. My grandad asked me to fix the roof!'" Harry muttered to himself. "They're all slimy!" he said, scrunching up his nose.

"Thirty quid buys you an awful lot of pies and comics." Grandad smiled.

"Fine," Harry said before taking a deep breath and blowing the dead leaves out of the gutter. Not only did the leaves fly, but Harry took out a few roof tiles and next door's washing as well. There were pants everywhere! "Oops, sorry, I'll put them

back." Harry said, zooming to the ground, picking up the tiles before flying back up and reattaching them to the roof. "There we go. All fixed! I'm not going next door

and messing with Mr Anderson's pants, though," Harry clarified. "Any more odd jobs you need doing?"

"No, I think it's safer if you don't do any more chores..." Grandad said, still unable to believe his eyes. "So, what now? Do you go and fight crime or something?" Grandad looked impressed, as Harry landed in the garden again.

"I don't know. I mean, I guess that's the thing to do. According to the books."

"The books?"

"Yeah, my comics. You get super-powers and then you fight crime... Oh no!" Harry exclaimed, looking at his grandad.

"What?"

"The comics I bought. I left them behind."

"At the warehouse?"

"My bus ticket, too," Harry said, patting his pockets in panic. "They'll be able to work out where I live!" Harry moaned, the blood draining from his face. "They'll be after us!"

5 p.m.

"Agent G! I think I found something..." The woman held up the carrier bag that Harry had left at the scene.

"Good one, Agent S," the man said, coming over to examine the evidence.

"What's the damage?" Agent S asked, looking at the mess Harry had made.

"The laser's OK. We can clear up the water. What do we have here?" said Agent G, peering in the bag, "Comics, a receipt from that shop around the corner – and a Number 14 bus ticket – a return from Wesley Avenue. Perfect." He smiled. "We'll have him within the hour."

"But now he has the … gift – I mean, all those powers – how will we catch him?" the woman asked.

"He's just a kid… Yes, he's got superpowers but he doesn't know how to use them. It's like sticking a Ferrari engine on a lawnmower. At the end of the day, all you have is an out-of-control lawnmower."

"I hope you're right. But what if this gets out? Why do you think he broke into the lab in the first place? Do you think he knows what we do here?" Agent S looked around nervously.

"I don't know. I have about a million

questions for him, too," Agent G said. "Let's go to the comic shop – they may be able to give us a name."

"Yeah, I know this kid. He's a regular," the woman behind the counter said, looking at the receipt. "He was in here earlier. I know everyone. I'm Frankie, of 'Frankie's Comics'. Wait a second, who are you guys?"

"Police," Agent G said, flashing a badge.

"Is he in trouble?"

"Oh no," Agent S said reassuringly. "We just wanted to return his comics. He left them on the bus and, well, someone got in touch with us."

"Wow, that's quite a service! The police getting involved so that some lad can have his comics back. Boy, he's going to give you guys a big hug!"

"Not if we get our hands on him … I mean, hug him first!" Agent S laughed.

"I'm surprised he forgot his comics, though," Frankie said curiously, taking a swig of her cherry slushy. "I mean, he's a bit of a nerd, if you know what I mean." Frankie gave a snort and almost choked, sticky red ice dribbling down her chin.

"It takes one to know one!" Agent G grinned.

"Yeah!" Frankie laughed. "Wait … what?"

"So, do you have an address for him?" Agent S ignored her, changing the subject.

"Erm, sure, I had to send him a couple of comics one time. Here it is: Harry Ramsbottom, 31 Wesley Avenue."

"I know it." Agent G smiled to himself.

"I notice you have CCTV in here." Agent S looked at the mini-camera above the cash till.

"Well, you can never be too careful. It all gets recorded here," she said, tapping her computer.

"Very wise." Agent G nodded. "Well, we'd better be off now," he said, holding out his hand to say goodbye. "Ooops!" he smirked as he knocked the slushy off the counter and all over the computer. It sparked and short-circuited in front of Frankie's eyes.

"Oh, I'm so sorry!" Agent G said. "I hope you haven't lost the CCTV?"

"What do you think? It's kaput!" Frankie said furiously.

"Maybe this will help repair it." Agent S said, handing over a stack of cash.

"Wow ... well ... yes ... that should do it." Frankie looked impressed. "Who knew the police were so kind?!" she called as Agent S and Agent G left.

"POLICE?!"

someone outside the shop shrieked. "Good! Something threw up all over me!" cried a very sticky and very stinky traffic warden. "I've never seen such a big pigeon!"

"Call 999." Agent G walked straight past and headed to the car. "We need to be somewhere," he said, as he threw Harry's comics into the bin.

"I leave you alone for a couple of hours and you've got two secret agents trying to kill you," Grandad said, shaking his head. "It might be time to rethink your shopping trips on a Saturday. They're becoming precarious."

"Now is not the time for a word of the day, Grandad," Harry groaned. "What do we do? We need a plan. What's the plan?!" Harry peeked nervously out of the front window, looking for danger signs.

"Why are you asking me?" Grandad seemed puzzled.

"Because you're a grown-up. Grown-ups are meant to have all the answers."

"No, they don't. We just pretend we do. To fool kids."

"What?"

"Well, you were going to find out one day." Grandad shrugged. "We're generally as clueless as you are; we just pretend to know what we're doing."

"Oh, well, that is just great," Harry sighed.

"Look, I don't know why you think you need my help. It's the other way round."

"What?" Harry asked.

"Listen, you're the expert in all this superhero stuff. You know what to do – it's in every comic you've ever read. It's all in there," Grandad said, tapping Harry's head.

Grandad was right: Harry had read hundreds, maybe even thousands, of stories about superheroes.

"We just need to follow the rules," he said.

"What rules?" Grandad asked.

"Well, for one thing, I'll need a sidekick," Harry said, looking at Grandad.

"Me?"

"Yep, you're in this as deeply as I am," Harry confirmed. "Obviously, we'll need some cool names and a logo – but we can worry about those later. First things first: we need to get out of here, and pronto. The agents know what I look like, so we need disguises. I mean, proper ones – wearing glasses and parting your hair on the other side doesn't count, Superman."

Then Harry had a eureka moment:

"WE NEED TO GO BACK TO THE WAREHOUSE!"

he shouted. "They won't look for us there. Returning to the scene of the crime; it's perfect..."

"Are you sure?" Grandad said, sounding sceptical.

"Yes, it's in every comic book. The place where it *all* starts is always where it *all* ends." Harry smiled. "Now for the disguises. How do you hide a superhero?" Harry pondered the question for a few moments. "I know: we'll dress as superheroes! They'll be expecting us to keep a low profile. They won't be looking for someone dressed like a superhero; it's the perfect double bluff. That's another rule: there has to be a lot of double-bluffing."

"And where am I going to rustle up a costume?" Grandad asked.

"You must have something suitable, Grandad."

"Hang on!" Grandad said, running to the cupboard and pulling out a box.

"What's this?" Harry said.

"Dust sheets – you know, for decorating. Basically, old curtains."

Harry pulled one out. It was lime green with big purple stripes. "I suppose it'll have to do," Harry said, looking at it, trying to imagine a time when this sort of thing was fashionable.

6 p.m.

"Well, what do you think?" Grandad said, pulling on his mask and admiring their creations in the mirror. "Pretty good disguises, eh?"

"Only if we happen to be hiding in a rainbow. Look at us!" Harry stared at the multicoloured paint-splattered outfits. "And my trousers are loose," Harry whined.

"That's the beauty of the curtain pant!"

Grandad said, pulling the cord and drawing Harry's trousers together like a pair of curtains.

"OW ... OW ... OW!"

Harry said.

"Sorry, too tight?" Grandad cut Harry a bit of slack in his slacks.

"Remember, if anyone asks, we're on our way to a fancy-dress party," Harry said. "Now, let's get out of here." He peered around the curtain. "Whoa…" He gulped, diving to the floor. "I think I just saw the same car as before."

"Back door?" Grandad asked.

"No." Harry shook his head. "One of the agents will go round the back."

"How are we going to get out of here?!"

"Up!" Harry said, bolting up the stairs. "Come on!"

Harry and Grandad ran all the way up to the top of the house. Harry peeked out of the window. Sure enough, the two agents were getting out of the car – *still* in dark glasses, *still* looking like they wanted to lock Harry up for the rest of his life.

Grandad spied them out of the window, too. "Blimey, you weren't kidding, were you? They look terrifying."

Harry and Grandad watched as the man went to the front door and the woman went round the back. "Told you," Harry said, opening the window.

"WHOA! YOU CAN'T GO OUT THERE – WHAT IF YOU FALL?" Grandad grabbed Harry's arm.

"SHH! I won't fall. I can fly, remember?"

"What am *I* supposed to do?" Grandad asked.

"You're coming with me," Harry said.

"WHAT IF *I* FALL?"

"I'll catch you."

"You'll catch me? I've seen you play cricket," Grandad said. "No way. You can't make me go out there."

"Yes, I can," Harry replied, grabbing Grandad by his cape.

"Darn your super strength!" Grandad said helplessly as they scrambled out the window and clung onto the roof.

"Shhh!" Harry said. "No screaming!"

"Why would I scream?" Grandad asked.

Harry held Grandad tightly by the hand and they soared into the air.

"AAAAAGHRRRRRR!!!" Grandad began screaming before quickly clamping his free hand over his mouth.

"Did you hear something?" Agent G asked Agent S on the radio.

"I did but there's nothing unusual here," she said, peering over the garden fence.

"Won't they see us?" Grandad asked. "I mean, flying people is a little obvious… Oh my word, this is amazing!" he said, trying not to squeal with delight.

"I've got an idea." Harry looked around. "We'll catch a ride!" he said, spotting an aeroplane flying by.

Harry waited for the right second then zoomed upwards to catch the tail wing of an EasyPlane flight back from Málaga. Agent G and Agent S looked up as the sound of the plane roared above, Harry and Grandad hidden from sight at the back of it.

"YOU SEE? EASY!" Harry said.

"WHOOOO HOOOO!
I'M SURFING ON A PLANE!"

Grandad whooped.

"Time to say goodbye," Harry said, and they jumped off. "Prepare for landing!"

"WHY CAN'T WE JUST FLY TO THE WAREHOUSE?"

"BECAUSE IT'S IN THE OTHER DIRECTION AND PEOPLE MIGHT JUST NOTICE A BOY AND HIS GRANDAD FLYING THROUGH THE SKY! WE'D BE ALL OVER SOCIAL MEDIA WITHIN SECONDS – AND WHO DO YOU THINK WILL BE MONITORING ALL OF THAT?"

"THE BAD GUYS?"

"EXACTLY. NO, LET'S WALK."

"WALK?! THAT'S SO BORING!"

"WALKING WAS FINE FOR YOU UP UNTIL ABOUT FOUR MINUTES AGO. THE MOST IMPORTANT THING IS TO KEEP A LOW PROFILE!" Harry shouted.

"YOU KNOW, NOT DRAW any attention to ourselves." Harry lowered his voice as they came in to land on the high street next to a burger van. "Just act casual."

"OK, but you do know we're wearing curtains?" Grandad huffed, trying to catch his breath while picking the flies out of his teeth.

"It's a Saturday night. We'll blend right in." Harry grinned at the sight of several suspicious-looking characters queued up by the cash machine, preparing for a night on the town. "Look, I can see three Spider-Men and several Catwomen already."

"And a bank robber, too!" Grandad pointed as a man with a balaclava – and what looked like a gun – walked to the front of the line.

"Oh, yeah!" Harry smiled. "Very convincing ... hang on, wait a second!"

"GET DOWN, OR YOU'LL GET IT!"

the bank robber yelled at the security guard who was loading the bank's takings into a van.

"That's not a costume!" Grandad said. "What are you going to do?" he asked Harry.

"Me? Why me?"

"This is what you superhero guys do! There's crime that needs fighting – right here in front of our eyes! You can't just do nothing."

"He's got a gun!" Harry said, crouching behind a postbox.

"SOMEONE DO SOMETHING!" a girl shrieked as the rest of the early-evening revellers saw what was happening.

"I could call the police," Harry said shakily to Grandad. "Can I borrow your phone?"

"*I can* call the police! Anyone can do that! If I had superpowers, I'd fly over there and give him a taste of his own medicine – you know, throw him a kung fu *thwack* or two. If you don't do something, one of those wannabe superheroes will! Just because they have the costumes, it doesn't make them invincible. You need to be decisive."

"Grandad, now is not the time for one

of your words of the day."

"That's just a regular word! My point is: they'll end up hurt. Or worse. Do you really want that on your conscience?"

Just as he said that, one of the Spider-Men cried out, "I'LL SAVE YOU!" and stumbled over towards the bank robber.

Grandad raised an eyebrow at Harry.

"Fine, I'll save the day! Happy now?" Harry took a deep breath and

WHOOOOOOORRRR!

he blew the Spider-Man off his feet and away from danger.

Harry thought for a moment – he just needed a bit of superpowered confidence. Muttering, "Nothing to worry about; it's just a man with a big gun…" under his breath, Harry walked over to the robber. "Excuse me… EXCUSE ME! Mr Robber!" Harry called out. "I wondered if you can help me?"

7 p.m.

"WHAT?" The armed robber turned around to face Harry.

"Sorry to interrupt, but I always fancied being an armed robber. Are you taking anyone on?"

"What *are* you talking about?" the armed robber said, looking utterly confused.

"I mean, what a great job!" Harry said, thinking on his feet. "The pay is great; the hours are pretty good, too. It's something that you can do anywhere. In many ways, it's ideal."

"HEL-LO! I'M ROBBING THIS GUY HERE! SORRY, I DON'T KNOW YOUR NAME, MATE." The robber pointed at the security guard who was cowering on the ground.

"Guy Mate," he answered.

"What?"

"My name's Guy Mate."

"Weird…" the robber remarked. "I've forgotten what I was saying… No, it's gone completely."

"I hate it when that happens," Guy frowned. "So annoying."

"So, anyway … maybe, I could be your apprentice," Harry said. "I could put things in bags or wave the gun around."

"Oh no!" the robber replied. "Guns are dangerous. I'd never have a real gun. I made this one out of wood."

"No way! That's made of wood!" Harry said, reaching for the gun.

Guy got up off the floor and the three of them stood around admiring the robber's handiwork.

"It took me ages. Truth be told, I'm pretty proud of it," the robber said, looking at the gun lovingly.

"You'd never know. To be honest, I was pretty scared for a second there. I really thought you had a gun," Guy said, impressed.

"So, can you hand over all the money please, Guy?" the robber said, pulling out a massive bag with "SWAG" written on the side.

"You know what? I don't think so," Guy said.

"Please, or I'll shoot you," the robber said.

"No, you won't. Not with a wooden

gun. I mean it's good, but it's not that good!" Guy chuckled.

"Well..." the robber said. "Maybe I could hit you with it?"

Before the robber could grab the gun, Harry threw it in the air, over the building and into outer space.

"What on earth? That's some throw you've got!" said Guy.

"I'm going to have to make another one now," the robber whined.

"I don't think they'll let you do that in prison." Harry said, pointing to the ten police cars that had turned up – along with a TV crew and about hundred passers-by, who were all filming it on their phones.

"So you don't really want to be an armed robber?" the robber said, looking rather sadly at Harry.

"Nah, I'm thinking about being a writer – either that or a YouTuber. This is just a bit of research really," Harry said nonchalantly.

"YouTuber? At least mine is a real job," the robber huffed. "Kids today, eh?"

At that, the police pounced on the robber, cuffed him and led him away to a life inside. Harry bowed to huge applause from the crowd.

"That was amazing!" Grandad smiled approvingly. "You saved the day."

"We need to go," Harry whispered, looking at all the cameras. "This isn't exactly the low profile I had in mind." But

before there was time to escape, a blood-curdling scream filled the air.

"AAAAARRRRRRGH!"

Harry, like everyone else, turned round to see where the noise was coming from.

A woman was shrieking in the middle of the crowd and pointing off into the distance. "There's an out-of-control school bus hurtling towards that home for orphaned kittens, the one between the fireworks factory and the match factory.

"SOMEONE DOOOOO SOMETHING!"

she yelled.

"Oh, come on!" Harry snapped. "I didn't even know Basingstoke had a fire-works factory!" Behind him, everyone was frozen in horror as the bus hurtled along the road with terrifying speed – one tyre had burst and the brakes were screeching like fingernails down a blackboard. Harry looked over at Grandad – who was raising his eyebrows at him.

"Oh, fine!" Harry sighed. He took a deep breath before flying like an arrow towards the bus.

"Is it a bird?!" a woman asked.

"Is it a plane?!" another gasped.

"No ... it's the boy who stopped the robbery. I'd recognize

that pair of curtains anywhere," someone else clarified.

Harry flew through the air as fast as he could. The bus was coming towards him at incredible speed. His eyes suddenly became like telescopes, zooming in on the terrified driver. It was like whatever his body needed in any given moment became a superpower – super parping power with the bin, super flying speed to escape the baddies, super confidence with the bank robber…

Harry could see the bus was full of screaming kids, which was a bit weird for a Saturday, but there you go. He swooped down, closed his eyes and stretched out his hands to cushion the impact as the bus came towards him.

"NO BRAKES!" the driver yelled.

"I gathered," Harry managed to answer back, his face squished against the windscreen. "What about handbrake, or reverse?"

"Nope." The driver shrugged.

"What does work?" Harry asked.

"Ow ... OW ... OW...!"

"The windscreen wipers," the driver said as they hit Harry in the face.

"PLEASE TURN THEM OFF!"

Harry dug his feet into the road, using himself as the brakes.

"Hot ... HOT!" Harry looked down as his feet began to billow with smoke.

"IT'S WORKING!" the driver cried as the bus began to slow down.

The bus screeched and lurched from side to side against Harry's super strength. Harry looked behind him as the large building that housed the orphaned kittens grew bigger and bigger. Was he about to be squashed? As if that wasn't enough, he felt like he was about to catch fire for the second time that day. There was one last screech as Harry dug his feet even harder into the road, making long skid tracks through the tarmac.

"WAAAAAAAAAAAAAAAAH!" he yelled. And it worked. The bus stopped, with centimetres to spare. Harry had saved the bus full of kids and the orphaned kittens – all without igniting the fireworks factory.

He let out a huge sigh of relief, which turned into a loud scream:

"WAAAAH! SOOO HOOOOOT!"

Harry ran in circles, his shoes smoking like a couple of chimneys, before spotting the fountain in the town square and jumping in head first. There was a huge sizzle, like when you spill milk on a hot stove, as his smoking feet hit the water.

"OH MY DAYS!" Harry said, his head rising above the water. "That's better!" Rubbing his eyes, he saw the crowd surrounding him: all with open mouths, all filming him, all trying to comprehend what they'd seen, what he'd just done. "Anywaaaay..." Harry smiled as he emerged, dripping wet. "See you around. Gotta fly!" He took off into the sky again, grabbing Grandad's hand as he went.

"Did he just steal a pensioner?" the robber asked. "And you say *I* belong in jail..."

8 p.m.

"That was amazing!" Grandad roared with delight as they zoomed away into the night sky. Harry looked behind them; cameras and flashing lights looked back.

"And we're flying again!" Grandad whooped with happiness.

"Yes, well, Operation: Sneaking Through the Town Unnoticed didn't quite go to plan, did it?" Harry grumbled.

"You were amazing," Grandad said,

laughing. "This is amazing! Everything is amazing!"

"Now where's a word of the day when you need one?" Harry laughed.

"You are really good at this! Listen, why don't you just accept it? This is your new life – we could be rich!" Grandad shouted.

"How will being a superhero make us rich?" Harry asked.

"Well, you could charge by the hour. Or maybe by distance – you know, if there's an emergency on the other side of the world. You could charge for each mile you have to fly."

"I'm not a black cab!" Harry said. "And what if someone who doesn't have much money needs me? Do I only help rich people?"

"OK, well, what about endorsements? You could be sponsored by an expensive brand."

"What … 'This life-saving rescue from a burning building was brought to you in association with Tesco's – because every little helps'?'" Harry asked.

"OK, maybe not rich, but you could be famous. Who doesn't want to be famous?" Grandad asked.

"I don't!" Harry protested. "Imagine not being able to do anything or go anywhere without people wanting this, that or the other from you? No, thanks! I like saving people, I like helping, but this superhero business isn't for me. I'm a kid. All I want to do is go back to my normal life – one where people aren't constantly filming me and where various parts of my anatomy don't catch on fire." Harry looked down at his still-smoking trainers. "I mean, these are ruined – my favourite pair! No thank you! And think of everyone who's after me. Not only have I got those secret agents chasing me for my superpowers, but now I have the media and the police too! Look, there's a helicopter following us now. Oh, this is just perfect ... now

I feel sick … all this flying around has made me feel bilious."

"All I am saying is that this is pretty cool! Being a superhero is cool! You did great things tonight; you saved people's lives. If I had your powers…" Grandad looked wistfully at Harry.

"THIS IS THE POLICE,"

the helicopter boomed out from its tannoy. "PLEASE PUT THE PENSIONER DOWN. STEALING OLD PEOPLE IS AGAINST THE LAW!"

Harry sighed. This always happened with superheroes. The police think they're bad guys and turn against them. It happens every time.

"I'M NOT BEING STOLEN! WE'RE

RELATED!" Grandad shouted back to the helicopter, trying to explain. "We like each other." Grandad gave Harry a squeeze.

"Look at that poor pensioner – he's clinging on for dear life," the helicopter pilot said to his co-pilot.

"You were right," Agent S said to Agent G, pulling out her phone. "They couldn't stay undercover for long." News of Harry's adventures had spread across social media and the story had been picked up by international TV channels.

"What's he been up to?" Agent G asked.

"Saving a bus full of kids as well as a rescue centre full of orphaned kittens, and foiling an armed robbery, so it seems." Agent S smiled.

"Perfect … he's perfect! Who'd have thought it? We just need to find him before anyone else does," Agent G said.

"That's not going to be easy – the police and every news channel in the world wants to know who he is – and the old man. They've even got a name for him – Smoky the Curtain Boy," Agent S said. "I think it has something to do with his feet and his costume."

"That may be the worst name I've ever heard," Agent G replied with a snigger. "We can get rid of that as soon as he's working for us. Now all we need to know is where to find him."

"He's being followed by a police helicopter." Agent S pointed at the location on her phone.

"Of course!" Agent G said.

"What?" Agent S asked.

"Look where he's heading." Agent G pointed on the map.

"Back to our base?" Agent S said. "Why?"

"He wants answers," Agent G said, as they got in the car and sped off down the road. "He's smart. He'll be perfect for what we need … once the tests are complete … once we have perfected the formula for the laser," he stared straight ahead. "Now let's capture ourselves a Smoky the Curtain Boy!" The name broke his concentration and he smirked again. "No, it's still the worst name I've ever heard."

"Step on it!" hollered Agent S. "We'll be there any moment."

“Cool, we’ve outflown a helicopter,” Grandad said, trying not to sound too impressed. “Well, you have. I didn’t do much, except wave.”

“Yes, it looked like you really wanted help – thanks for that. They think I’ve kidnapped you now. Let’s land – I’m getting tired,” Harry said as they came to a stop outside the mysterious warehouse near the comic shop. “Watch out for a cat,” Harry added. “I blame him for this whole thing.”

“So this is where you got zapped?” Grandad asked. “I always wondered what this place was. I thought it was a bingo hall.”

Harry raised his eyebrows and pointed

at the razor-sharp fence and security cameras. He took one breath and blew the cameras off their posts. "Yeah, right," he said. "Come on, this way."

Harry ran round the side of the building to the back. The door was still partly open from where he'd crawled in and out. This time, though, Harry lifted the metal shutter like it was made of paper.

"In here," Harry said.

"It's so dark. Let me find a light switch," Grandad said.

"No!" Harry snapped. "That's how this whole thing got started." He squinted into the dark. "Hang on..." Just as he thought about seeing in the dark, everything suddenly came into focus. Harry left his grandad surrounded in gloomy shadows.

"Harry!" Grandad called.

"There we go!" Harry said, flicking a switch on the desk lamp in the corner. He picked up some papers marked *TOP SECRET* on the desk. "Hey!" he said.

"What is it?" Grandad asked.

"Operation Mongoose, apparently." Harry quickly scanned the files. "It looks like these are plans to use a human in an experiment – to turn him or her into a superhero who would, quote, 'help do the agency's work'." Harry paused. "What do you think that means?"

"I don't know, but it doesn't sound good," Grandad said, taking out his

glasses for a closer look.

"It says here that 'the subject of the testing' – that's me, I presume – will 'spend the rest of their life working for the agency, obeying orders and making the agency the most powerful organization in the world'." Harry gulped. "These *are* master criminals, Grandad. I've been zapped and now they want to own me for ever."

9 p.m.

"What do we do?" Grandad asked.

"There's only one thing for it," Harry said, twirling his cape. "If I'm not a superhero, they can't make me work for them. You'll have to reverse the process – unzap me, if you will."

"What? How?"

"With the laser!" Harry nodded towards to the lever.

"You want me to unzap you with a

laser? Wouldn't that just give you an extra zap?!" Grandad said, trying to keep up.

"Do you have a better idea? It must be the only way to cancel it all out. Come on! You need to fire it at my bottom."

"I'm not sure I'm comfortable with this, Harry."

"You've got plenty of experience at this sort of thing," Harry said, running over and pulling the lever. A familiar rumble and whine started as the huge laser powered up.

"What are you talking about?" Grandad said. "I have no experience of firing lasers at anyone, let alone precise parts of their body."

"Come on," Harry said. "You used to work with lasers."

"I used to scan barcodes when I was a delivery driver. I didn't work for NASA."

"Oh, it's the same thing. Just think of my bottom as a giant barcode!" Harry yelled encouragingly.

"That's a *really* weird sentence!" Grandad yelled back, running over to the machine. "How do we make it reverse the powers?" Grandad asked, looking at it nervously. "This all looks very complicated. Remember, it took me two years to get my Sky Box to work properly."

"Well, I was hoping for a giant dial that you could switch to reverse … if this was a comic that's what would happen." Harry peered at the screen next to the laser as it bleeped and flashed various percentages:

Strength 100%
Flying Ability 100%…

"What if this doesn't work and I fry you to toast?" Grandad said.

"Well, that's why it's very important that it does work! Look, it says here that all my powers are on a hundred per cent. Now, if we turn each of these dials down

to zero, then that will reverse it, right?"

"That sort of makes sense. I suppose," Grandad agreed as Harry set about twiddling the dials. "But on the other hand…"

"What?" Harry said.

"What if you just disappear? That'd be turning everything down to zero, too. Literally!" Grandad called over the noise of the machine as it revved up, growing louder and louder. "We need more time to think," Grandad said. "Maybe there are some instructions in those drawers? People always have a drawer stuffed with instructions."

"This isn't a toaster from Currys PC World, you know. It doesn't come with a helpline. This stuff is from another planet … probably!" Harry said pointedly.

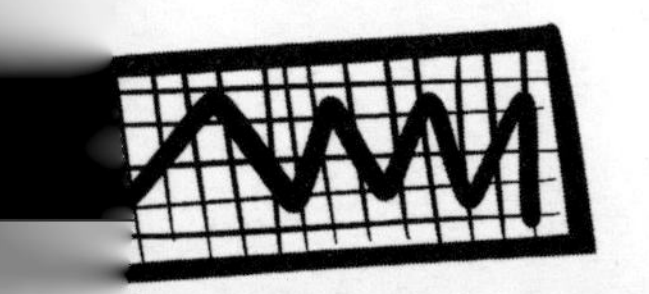

"OK, let's just stop this thing. It sounds angry!" Grandad shouted. "I'll press the red button. Red always means 'stop', right?"

Before Harry could answer, Grandad had hit the button.

"Thirty seconds until firing," came a robotic voice.

"OR sometimes it means 'fire', too!" Harry yelled. "Especially on big evil machines. You must never, ever press the big red button!"

"Twenty-nine … twenty-eight…"

"OK, so that's my bad," Grandad said. "How do we turn it off?"

"Certainly not by pressing random buttons! This is why your Sky Box only ever records stuff with subtitles," Harry said.

"Twenty-five ... twenty-four..."

"Are the dials turned down to zero?" Grandad shouted.

"Yes! Just point it at my bottom," Harry hollered back.

"But what if you're wrong?!" Grandad screamed.

"But what if I'm right?"

"But what if you're not?"

"BUT WHAT IF I AM?!"

"That's not really a sound argument," Grandad said. "It's a false dichot—"

"GRANDAD, ENOUGH WITH THE BIG WORDS! I'M DOING THIS! FIRE IT AT MY BOTTOM! DOOOOO IIIIIT!" Harry cried.

Grandad took aim and zapped. Harry jumped a metre into the air and then...

The machine ground to a halt and shut down.

"I don't think so...!" Agent G said, his hand on the lever. Harry and Grandad looked round at the two agents.

"Grandad, run!" Harry screamed. "Thiiiiis way!"

They bolted up some nearby steps which led to a metal platform high above the floor of the laboratory. A series of stairs and corridors zigzagged beneath the platform weaving like a snake towards the ground below.

"Lock all the doors, Agent S!" Agent G said.

"Already done," she responded, pressing a button on her phone.

Harry reached the end of the corridor but it was a dead end. They were trapped! He turned around and saw what looked like a fire escape on the platform below. "C'mon, Grandad! It's our only chance." With that, he took a giant leap and landed. He turned round to see Grandad vaulting the handrail...

"WAAAH!"

Grandad yelled as he missed the platform. He hung on by his fingernails to the railing. "Leave me, son. You go – it's you they're after."

"No!" Harry said. "I still have my powers. I'm not going to let you go!" Harry reached over and grabbed Grandad by the hand. "Oh no…" Harry said, struggling to pull his grandad up.

"What?" Grandad asked.

"My powers, they're draining away," Harry said. "Must doooo it!" Harry pulled with all his might. "MUST DO IT!" Harry gritted his teeth and lifted Grandad high enough to heave him to safety.

"You saved my life!" Grandad whimpered. "I love you, Harry."

"I love you, too, Grandad… Now, let's get out of here before these two kill us."

"I'm sorry … what?" Agent G said.

"You heard!" Harry said, opening the door to make his escape.

"They know that's where we keep the tea and biscuits, right?" Agent S said, watching as Harry and Grandad ran into the store cupboard. A second later, Harry and Grandad casually strolled back out.

"Sorry, could you tell us how to escape? We're lost," Harry said, smiling awkwardly.

"Listen, no one is going to kill you. We've been trying to help you," Agent S said.

"Gavin, why don't you put the kettle on."

"Good idea, Sue," the other agent said. "I'm parched and I think we've got some explaining to do."

"Gavin and Sue?" Harry said.

10 p.m.

"You mean, you're not baddies?" Grandad asked.

"No, like I said, we've been trying to help you," Agent G said. "We knew you'd been accidentally shot with the laser and we wanted to make sure you were all right."

"Well, you dress like baddies and you act like baddies!" Harry said suspiciously.

"Another biscuit?" Agent S asked.

"Lovely. Thank you." Harry smiled.

"The black suits and grim expressions – it's just expected in our line of work," Agent G said, dunking his biscuit in his tea.

"What is your line of work?" Grandad asked.

"We work for MI10," he replied.

"Hang on. I've heard of MI6 and MI5 – but what do MI10 do?"

"We're a super-secret organization that fights crime using experimental techniques."

"Like lasers from outer space?" Harry asked.

"Outer space? No, I built this – it took me ages!" Agent S said. "Who said it was from outer space?"

"A guy who read it on the Internet…" Harry said.

"*Of course.* No, this is all human-made," Gavin added. "Our plan was to create a superhuman to fight crime by blasting a volunteer with a laser, boosting their cellular structure and giving them superpowers. That's why we wanted to talk to you – to make sure you were OK and to see what you could do."

"By locking me up in a cage and carrying out tests on me day and night, no doubt?!" Harry exclaimed.

"No, we were going to use a questionnaire," Sue said, holding out a clipboard and biro.

"Oh … but it says in there that the superhero would have to obey orders!" Harry pointed to the paperwork he'd found.

"Well, yes, that's how MI10 works. There are orders, like, 'Can you stop that bus crashing into a fireworks factory?' or 'Stop that armed robber!' The idea was that our hero would carry them out, the world would be safer, then we could have some tea and biscuits."

"What about the rest of MI10? Would they offer me tea and biscuits?" Harry asked. "Or would they lock me away like a superhero freak for the rest of my life?!"

"There's only Sue and myself," Gavin said.

"I told you we were secretive," Sue said. "We would have paid you, obviously. You would have had holidays. And we'd have come up with a better costume and name for you, too."

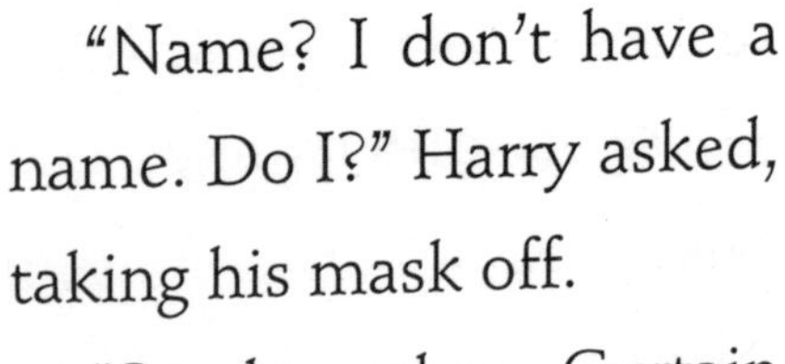

"Name? I don't have a name. Do I?" Harry asked, taking his mask off.

"Smoky the Curtain Boy, according to social media," Gavin said, breaking the news.

Harry scrunched up his face like he'd been sucking on a lime and shook his head.

Gavin gave him a sympathetic look and carried on. "If you agree to come and work for us, then we'd need to laser you again and make sure your powers are permanent. Will you, Harry?"

"Permanent, you say?" Harry asked.

"Yes, you got a mini-zap. That laser is just a tester, really – to check the tech worked. We've been trying to find the perfect specimen to test, and, well, I guess you found us. If you come and join MI10, we'd use the proper laser," Gavin said, pressing a button on the desk. A laser, maybe thirty times the size of the first one, appeared from the ceiling.

"WHAAAAT?!
That's huge!"

"So, Harry, what do you say?" Agent S asked. "Do you fancy changing your life for ever?"

Several months later...

"Listen to me, you birdbrained nincompoop! If you take another step, I'll swat you like a fly from here to Japan, do you understand?"

"You're just a kid! How are you going to stop me from stealing this gold?"

"Don't push me, Evil Dr No Good. You're really starting to annoy me now. Today was supposed to be my birthday. I was going to spend it with my grandad."

"Birthday? You should have said! Here, let

me give you some cake – oh, and it wouldn't be a birthday without candles..." Evil Dr No Good pulled a huge red bomb from his bag and lit the fuse. "Now what are you going to do? Let this bomb go off with all those innocent people upstairs? Or fly away and defuse the bomb far from here ... meaning I am free to escape with the gold? MWAHAHA!"

"Neither," Danger Boy said, blowing out the fuse on the bomb. "You're not going to escape with that bag of gold, either."

"What?"

"Because it isn't gold in there!"

Evil Dr No Good opened up the bag. "No way. It's Silver Shadow!"

"It is, indeed. Drop your weapons! Nothing comes between Danger Boy and Silver Shadow and their birthday pie!"

"Not the old switcheroo... But how did they do it?" someone called.

An engrossed crowd stared up at the podium in the crammed comic shop.

"Well, I'll have to tell you in the next issue..." Harry had just finished reading aloud at the launch party of his bestselling comic series.

"Wow, he's

so good!" one audience member said to Frankie the owner.

"He's been coming here since he was tiny," Frankie said proudly. "Now look at him – he creates total comic hits! I don't know where he gets his ideas from."

"Who wants their comics signed?" Harry yelled to the excited crowd.

A couple of hours later, Harry was on his way home. He chuckled to himself, remembering how his first comic – the story of a boy who accidentally got zapped with superpowers – had been a massive hit. Every so often he thought about whether he'd made the right choice, giving it all up… Who wouldn't want to be a superhero? It was pretty exciting for a day, he admitted, but could he have done it for ever? No. It just wasn't him. It was like watching nature documentaries about lions – he loved them but would never want to actually be in one.

That's *really* how Harry felt about becoming a superhero – too much responsibility. All he had ever wanted was to be a writer and all he had needed was an idea – and now he had one. It all started when he wrote down what had happened to him and Grandad, changing some details so that MI10 wouldn't be discovered. And he found that although he'd lost his powers, he had somehow kept the confidence to write the words down on the page – and it didn't even matter about his spelling. It turns out you don't have to be a perfect speller to be an amazing writer! There'd been a few rumours initially that maybe he was the real Smoky the Curtain Boy superhero, who came and saved the town for one night before disappearing for ever. But, after a while, the whole evening's events became fuzzy, as if the whole thing had been a dream, and the world moved on.

MI10 managed to find their guinea pig in the end, someone willing to be shot by the real laser. The superhero works in secret these days, no costume made out of curtains. More like a shadow who quietly goes around stopping crime whenever and wherever he can.

"Hi, Grandad, I'm home," Harry said, walking through the door.

"Hey, Hal, how'd the new comic go down?"

"Brilliant, lots of copies sold. I think this one is going to do really well." Harry smiled, shutting the front door behind him. He took a deep breath. "Hmmmm, minced beef?"

"You knows it!" Grandad grinned. "Lay the table – it's almost ready."

A few minutes later, they sat down together in their new house. It was bigger than the last, with no dodgy guttering. It was nearer town, too – just a five-minute walk from the comic shop.

"Pass the gravy," Grandad said. But before Harry could hand it over, the phone rang. "Now, who's this...?" Grandad said, getting up and answering the phone. "OK ... OK ... be there in ten."

"What is it?" Harry asked.

"Put my pie in the oven, would you? There's work to be done!" Grandad said, putting on his mask. "The Silver Shadow is needed once more. Evil Dr No Good has escaped from prison."

"Don't forget – remember every detail, Grandad! I may need ideas for my next book. Oh, and say hello to Sue and Gavin for me." Harry waved his grandad goodbye.

"Affirmative. That means yes, by the way." Grandad winked before opening the window and jumping out into the night sky.

Harry watched as his grandad zoomed off into the distance, ready to save the day once again. Oh, yeah, MI10 found the right guy in the end. That was for sure.

READ MORE ME

Best friends Freddy and Sal have accidentally started a **SPACE WAR** with Alan, a grumpy alien brain muncher from planet Twang. Freddy is about to become the most famous kid in his town, for all the wrong reasons!

Pete is having the **WORST DAY EVER!** He's accidentally robbed a corner shop and now he must race against time to prove that he is not **THE MOST WANTED** boy in the world!

www.walker.co.uk

A ADVENTURES!

Billy is busy digging for treasure in the garden when he unexpectedly **OPENS A WORMHOLE** and all sorts of people from the past start to pop out. Billy must act fast before history is changed **FOR EVER!**

Molly decides to **BUILD A ROBOT** to do her homework. But her robot is pretty clever and it builds another robot to do it instead ... and then another. Now Molly must race against time to stop a **MEGA ROBOT INVASION!**

Create your own COMIC BOOK SUPERHERO in five easy steps!

Draw a circle for the face, with two small ears.

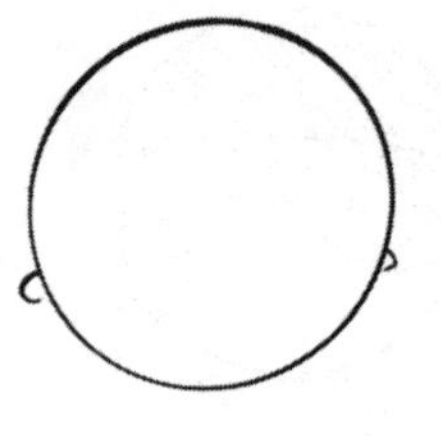

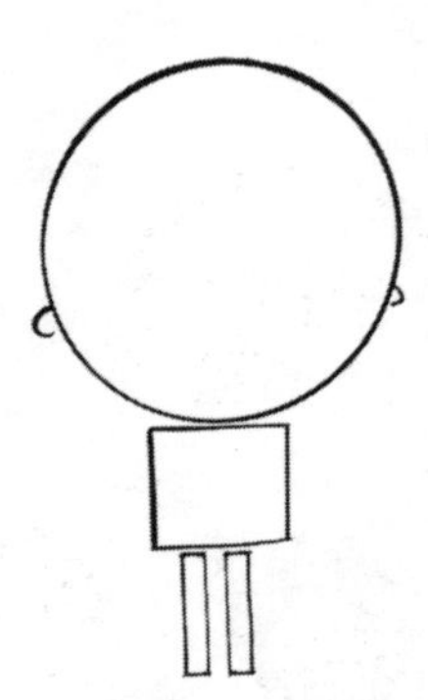

2

Create the body by drawing a big square and two small rectangles.

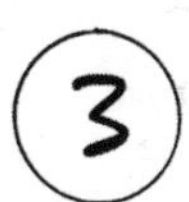

Add arms, hands, feet and your super-hero cape.

4

Give your superhero some facial features – eyes, nose, mouth, hair and a superhero mask.

Draw a thicker outline around the body shape and make your superhero fly by adding some clouds!

Roll the dice three times. For each roll, match the number to the word in the tables: A, then B, then C.

For example, if you roll a three, then a four, then a six, you'll get the name ELECTRO SPIDER LEGEND!

A

1	LASER
2	JUMPING
3	ELECTRO
4	LEAPING
5	SMOKIN'
6	DISCO

B

1	RAT
2	MONKEY
3	LION
4	SPIDER
5	PANDA
6	DINO

C

1	BOY
2	WOMAN
3	GIRL
4	DUDE
5	MAN
6	LEGEND

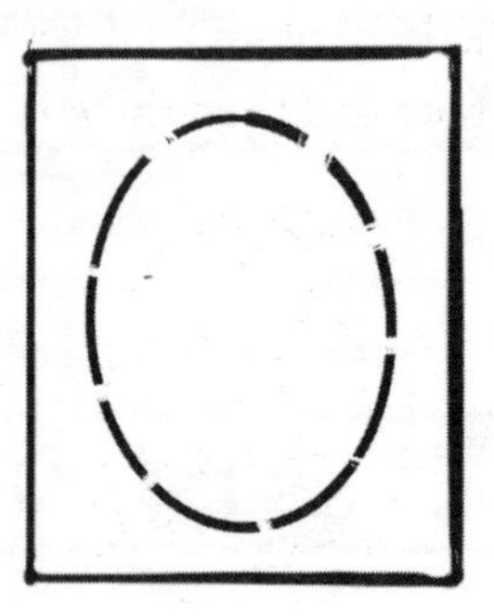

1. Take a piece of card and draw an oval.

2. Draw eyes, a nose and a mouth – with big fangs!

3 With the help of an adult, cut out the face and then the eyes.

4 Get painting!

5 Once your mask is dry, make two holes on either side and tie on some string to fix it to your head. Go, baddie!

Now you have your superhero and baddie characters, photocopy this comic strip template and draw your own superhero adventure!

My name's Tom, I'm the fella who wrote and illustrated the book (illustrated is just a posh way of saying I drew the pictures). I'm here to tell you a little bit about myself. I used to be a cartoonist for a newspaper, it was my job to draw cartoons of prime ministers and presidents. After that I started writing and illustrating my own books. I like football, fizzy sour sweets, laughing lots, sausages, staring out of the window and writing books. I have silly children, three wives and a lovely dog … no hang on, I mean I have a silly dog, three children and a lovely wife.

Find out more at **www.tommclaughlin.co.uk**

www.walker.co.uk